Sinister Emails
Thirty-Two Tactics for Tormenting

By Ricky Russ Jr

rickyruss.com

Reviews:

"A must-have collection of emails for those who desire to eternally control their marionette!"
~ Charles M

"With the end times quickly approaching, the timing for this timeless classic couldn't be more timely!"
~ Joseph S

"These daily emails are the best thing since records being played backward!"
~ Billy G

"Not since the invention of the glorious Pill has our world possessed such a wonderfully dark gift."
~ Bill C

"If it weren't for Sinister Emails, my partner would be living a j*yful and abundant l*fe. These tactics are truly sinister."
~ Anton L

"Because of Sinister Emails, I now feel like a member of a special legion of leaders. After only four days of implementing these tactics, my partner has already begun to isolate and speak negatively about other partners."
~ John K

"I bel*eve these crafty emails are our version of Good to Great. I've watched my partner go from bad to worse in less than a week. Thank you."
~ Beth M

"Wow. The email from Day 18 was worth the price of submission all by itself. I could literally see the evil dripping off the page."
~ Ernie M

"Mr. Sinister! You have done it again. At first, I didn't think you would ever top your previous inventions; including country music, the Hallmark channel, four-way stops, the Black Light, and mayonnaise. No wonder a third of he*ven followed you. Congrats!"
~ Joel O

Sinister Emails
The Remastered Book Edition

A few years ago, I was tagging along with my wife at an affluent estate sale in Wilsonville, Oregon. While she was rummaging around in their garage, I happened to stumble upon a shoebox full of old cell phones in their driveway.

When I asked the elderly woman who owned the house how much she wanted for the phones, she replied, "You can have the entire box for $50 because I don't know anything about cellular vices. I also don't know if any of them work, or if they need the Wi-Fis. After my late husband disappeared, I found an open safe in the closet just behind his custom shoe rack. Somehow, I never knew that safe was there. Anyway, that's where I found those old vices."

After I purchased the shoebox full of phones, I drove home and began checking to see if each device worked. There was one particular phone, a Blackberry, that still contained files on the Micro SIM card. Upon extracting these files onto my Airbook, I came across a zip file labeled *SE_32_TFT*.

After opening the folder, I discovered 32 images that looked as if someone printed off a series of emails, made edits, and then scanned each as a TIFF file. I can only assume, but it's possible they did all of this so that no record would be found on their personal email server. I'm not sure of the origin of these emails or the dates when these emails were captured, because that information has been crossed out.

For years I've hesitated to share these emails with anyone due to their sinister nature and the fact that the thirty-two tactics could be used for bad. However, I believe there is nothing hidden that won't be disclosed, and there is no secret that won't be brought out into the light.

The following pages contain each email.

Dear %%First Name%%,

Welcome to Sinister Emails. It's essential during your allotted time on earth that you remember the following information in regards to the partner you've been assigned to:

- You will never be able to physically touch your partner or harm him with any earthly object, but you can bury your tongue deep into his ear. Let your tongue be the creaking hammock that continually swings back and forth in his mind.

- You must multitask at all times. Keep copious notes on your partner's surroundings and the things he pays attention to so that you will have fuel for future torments.

- You won't be able to know your partner's future, but while he sleeps, you can visit the partners he keeps company with so that you can know his future from the plans they have regarding him.

- If you notice him experiencing any spiritual growth towards light, feel free to pile on a previous day's tactic for further tormenting.

- From the moment your partner wakes, until the moment he falls asleep, you must continuously be in his ear. Do not let his ears rest.

- You must completely understand the difference between flattery, compliment, and complement. Always complement tactics with flattery, but never allow your partner to compliment another partner.

- Lastly, and most importantly, you must always speak in the first person when you talk to him. **He must bel*eve ALL of his thoughts are his own.** If you whisper in his ear, "I am such a loser!", he might bel*eve it. If he bel*eves it, he might say it. And if he says it, well, he will start to live it.

WEEK 1

Day 1:
Onboarding & Mental Waterboarding

%%First Name%%, today is the foundational day to begin waterboarding your partner's pure little mind. From the time he wakes until he falls asleep, and even while he dreams, torment is the name of the game. You must be unrelenting with tormenting. There will be other days when you give him a short break only to make him think he's gained a moment of pe*ce and victory, but today is not that day. As long as today is called today, it's the opportune time to torment.

I trust you have dissected and memorized your partner's case file down to the very last entry. You are going to need every little piece of his past for today's onslaught. What will victory taste like, you ask? Divinely bitter. You'll know when your victory is nearing because you'll see him grab both of his ears while closing his eyes. He's doing this to mute out his surroundings. He still doesn't realize he's in a spiritual fight. However, while he's inwardly flailing about in this toddler-like behavior, pay close attention to what's right in front of him so that the moment he opens his eyes, you can thump him with thoughts from the visuals that enter his windows.

Remember, even though he's so much more powerful than you are, he doesn't know it. Feed on this. He's merely dragging through l*fe bel*eving he's weak, much like all of the other upright lemmings.

Like a noose, I want you to wrap our truths around his neck and connect them to his ears. Don't slumber for a moment no matter what. The goal for today is that he falls asleep tonight completely tormented so that he wakes up mentally hungover. If he wakes up the following morning in this condition, not even his highlighted scriptures will be able to save him from Day 2's tactics!

xxx†xxx

Today's Tactic: Any time your partner is trying to exercise what he calls humility by listening to others as opposed to talking, counter the talker's every word by whispering faultsaboutthatperson'sappearance. Like a moth to a flame, your partner will move from listening to hearing if he begins to judge! If you can get him to error twice in the same moment, you, my son, are doing a delightfully devious job.

SINcerely,
SINister
CEO • PsyD, EdD

Day 2:
Spontaneous & Rapid Insults

Good morning, %%First Name%%. Today's tactic is all about getting results with insults. However, we don't want your partner to ever say the insults audibly where anyone can hear him. The goal is for him to simply think on insults.

Again, you must speak in the first person so that he thinks less of himself because he's thinking these insults. The quicker you are on the draw with planting insults, the better. At the same time, you have to find a balance between using insults that are too soft and too cutting. We want him to slowly bleed out during the day without knowing it.

For example, if while his wife is speaking to him, you say, "I can't continue living with this pig any longer," he might wonder what made him think this thought? But if you say, "She is so illogical!", you can build on that over time. We have to stack these insults slowly. In essence, we want to build a mental house of insult cards that causes him to feel only disgust for her. If the very thought of his wife brings negativity to the surface, you win. There's nothing darker in a marriage than silent hatred growing like Toxicodendron radicans around his h*art.

We desire for the termites of contempt to slowly and silently chew away at the l*ve he has for her, thus leaving him in an isolated and empty house that reminds him of her. It's at this point you'll realize and know the power of one silent thought that you buried in his mind at the opportune time. Never underestimate the power of a couple of innocuous words repeatedly whispered throughout the day. While you might not see any growth from your sowing, be patient. All of these insults produce ongoing mental marathons over a period of time in which most partners can't endure.

Also, another great insult to inject is the insult of absence. Let me explain. Let's use his wife again as the example. If you can get your partner to never or hardly ever say, "I l*ve you.", then you have accomplished something truly remarkable. His wife longs to hear him say these three dreadful words, and the last thing we want is for her to experience even one minute of j*y.

So, here's how to keep your partner from mouthing a single kind word. Any time he's around her, whisper to him something like, "She knows I l*ve her. I don't have to say it."

Listen carefully to the things she says as well so that you can whisper the opposite to your partner. Remember, they both bel*eve in the power of the spoken word, and that's why it's paramount for your partner to keep quiet. Our data shows that the scheme of absence flies beneath their spiritual radar.

xxx†xxx

Today's Tactic: Because partners spend one-third of their l*fe at work, you will need tried-and-true marketplace tactics. Your partner bel*eves he should be the manager, much like most arrogant partners do. So, the best times to attack him during these time slots are on the way to work and then on the way home. You have his entire commute to deceptively roll out the red carpet of negativity in regards to his boss. Stack assumptions on top of assumptions. Remind him of past insults that were spoken to him. We want him to arrive at work with a tiny fuse, and we want him to drive home furiously focused on the explosion that manifested.

SINcerely,
SINister
CEO • PsyD, EdD

Day 3:
Socialpathic Media

Today is going to be a delightfully dark day, %%First Name%%. I think you're going to Like the angle on today's socio-strategy.

First, never give your partner the thought of deactivating any of his social media accounts nor fasting social for a season. We desire isolation in the home, but not isolation online. We want him soaking in social. In fact, we want him on social all the time, but not for posting. Yes, you read that correctly.

There are no *Top 10 Worst Words* for your partner to use in order to bully partners online. In fact, I don't want your partner posting anything online. Only our rookies who don't listen, attempt to get their partners to use the elementary tactic of posting.

Also, do whatever it takes to keep

him from typing encouraging things or posting anything that brings j*y to other partners. You can accomplish this by planting thoughts of doubt the very second you see him starting to post. Whisper things like, "What if someone reads this post the wrong way?", "What If someone thinks I'm bragging?", or "What if I don't get any Likes?" H*pefully, the thoughts you plant will cause him to erase what he started to type. If this happens, he might just continue down the meaningless and spiraling path of scrolling.

Do you remember what Judge Skroll said in his keynote that went fungal online? He said, "You can kill two doves with one bullet if you can get your partner to only scroll all day. If your partner is face-down and scrolling, he won't be engaged with the partners right in front of him. And, if he doesn't stop to post while scrolling, then you will have more time to lather demeaning thoughts of judgment on every post he sees."

Judge Skroll is the guru of this strategy. Learn from him. Use social as your tool.

Take note: It's not about the content that's posted; it's about the thoughts that take root in your partner's mind regarding his fellow partners' posts!

Now, if you can't detour your partner from posting, then you must bombard him with the nasty nuisance of notifications. Every time his phone buzzes, dings, or lights up, you have to immediately spray venom down his ear canal. You have to keep him preoccupied and in a constant state of doubt and worry. In an ideal kingdom, we would have a cortisol IV drip attached to his frontal lobe at all times. You need to mentally deplete and breakdown your partner with the aid of every social platform.

When it comes to other partners' posts, throw extra kerosine on the words written by his fam*ly members. We want each word that he reads to re-ignite the painful thoughts from his childhood. You have to get him to a place where comparison has taken up residence in the corner of his mind while endlessly stirring up dark thoughts of jealousy.

Don't spend any time inventing infectious words about social justice or political correctness; these are superficial and soon forgotten. Your focus has to be on the extraction of l*ve. If there's an ounce of dissension in your partner's h*art before he ever arrives at a fam*ly gathering, then your job will be easier while he's there.

xxx†xxx

Today's Tactic: Give him the idea to post a fam*ly photo on his social. This will seem harmless to him, but you will twist all the j*y out of it. Paint a poetic picture on his cranial canvas where everyone who views the photo is smiling. I know this sounds backward, but trust me, it's genius.

Here's why. If you can get him to post a fam*ly photo, then we can get other partners who view this photo to either be jealous or feel sadness.

Here's how. After the image is posted, we will target partners with fractured families to see your partner's photo, and we will douse the floor of their mind with shame the very moment they scroll to it. There's nothing more exhilarating than dividing families with false perceptions using another fam*ly member's l*ve.

SINcerely,
SINister
CEO • PsyD, EdD

Day 4:
The Illusion of Irreversible Identity

Good morning, Gnash! Sorry about the errors with your name in the previous emails. Our technical difficulties seem to never end. Speaking of names, today's email might be one of the most important ones I've blasted out to you.

Today, we will be covering a topic regarding your partner's spiritual identity. Our strategy with his identity is to keep him from ever discovering who he truly is. We can do this by repeatedly reminding him of all the titles that other partners have spoken to him over his l*fetime. Capitalize on this, especially if the time comes when another partner gets a glimpse of his true identity. If you see this happening, you will have to replace their words at a 10:1 ratio. Like the effects of a sizzling hot branding iron, we want false identity branded on every square inch of your partner's mind. If he has ever lost in a competition, you whisper, "I'm a loser." If he's ever cheated on his wife, you whisper, "I'm an adulterer." If he's ever gotten a DUI, you whisper, "I'm an alcoholic." If he has ever stolen, you whisper, "I'm a thief." You get the point, now point out his past. Make your partner feel smaller than a midget on his knees. If he makes a practice of bel*eving that he is what he does, then it's only a matter of time before we can get other partners to incarcerate him in our ever-growing mental health program.

We have lost countless lost partners over the centuries due to the tragic discovery of their true identity. While we can't figure out where this discovery is coming from, we are sure it has something to do with an ambiguous wind of some sort. If your partner discovers his true identity, and then begins to walk in it, horrendous things ensue - things such as j*y, h*pe, pe*ce, l*ve, forg*veness, and more. I can't continue listing all of the byproducts without being filled with rage. This is why we have to do everything in our power to flood your partner's mind with regrets from his past. Again, whenever true identity is discussed between partners, tormenting must be unrelenting; it must be an all-day onslaught of lies.

xxx†xxx

Today's Tactic: I don't know if you've noticed or not, but your partner currently owns a horrendous book called *Who I Am in Chr*st*.

Tonight, I want you to study this book inside and out while he sleeps. Towards the back, you will find a list of thirty-three sentences that are also located in his Book of lies. Although these sentences are complete trash, I still want you to memorize each one so that you can quote the opposite to him when he's not obeying your thoughts. And, I want you to quote the same sentences when he's in the middle of following your whispers as well. We want to drown him in condemnation and confusion.

When it comes to any thoughts about his true identity, he needs to bel*eve he IS a sinner. He needs to bel*eve he IS broken. He needs to bel*eve that nothing works together for good. He needs to bel*eve that he can be separated from G*d's l*ve. While all of the statements above are the complete opposite of what he reads in his Book of lies, you can replace his bel*efs using misdirection if you're persistent. Then, in the future, if he hears any partner proclaim one of these sentences, his soul will shiver from shame. Let's not grow weary in striving to wrap the cloak of darkness around his true identity. If we accomplish this feat, his roots will surely become diseased, and then he will be thrown to us.

SINcerely,
SINister
CEO • PsyD, EdD

Day 5:
Automatic Weapons

Good day, Gnash! I think you are really going to enj*y today's email. Because your partner has been brainwashed to avoid the obvious errors, he won't be able to detect the grenades you are about to roll in. Your partner has been trained to focus only on trivial matters we call automatic weapons. You know, things like guns, politics, and yoga pants. I h*pe you're reading between the lines with these examples. Leave him be during these times. Let him divide, bicker, and lust over these childish things.

While he's tiring himself out with these minuscule matters, you can use this time to plant better land mines in his mind. You have to be productive and efficient with your time whenever he is doing your work for you. So, while he invests his time focusing on automatic weapons, plan to ~~tear~~ tare up his fields.

The first land mine you can plant is the mine of fear. All of his automatic weapons breed fear regarding his future. He fears being killed. He fears being on the losing side. He fears being led astray by the leper with maggots in her mouth. Fear is a magnificent and malevolent mine because it means he's not living in the moment when he's focused on fear.

The second land mine you can plant is the mine of regret. There's a profound thought that was left out of a sentence in his Book of lies. If my memory serves me correctly, our one-time champion Paul, post-Damascus, wrote, "*blah. blah. blah. Neither death nor life. Nor things present. Not things to come...*" Gnash, do you not see what I don't see? Notice what he left out of his statement. He didn't include the partner's past along with his present and future.

This means you have a way in. This is your key. His past. His regret. If you just camp out all day and throw logs on the fires of his past, you might just be able to chain him in yesterday's solitary confinement!

xxx†xxx

Today's Tactic: If your partner doesn't receive a consistent paycheck, here's a tremendous tactic to use. Begin to build a maniacal story in your partner's mind about his future finances in h*pes of stirring up ongoing fear.

For example, if another partner places a check in the mail for your partner without telling him, you will have three days to paralyze your partner with every possible fear since he doesn't know the check is on the way. Flood him with thoughts of having to downsize his home, cancel certain bills, sell his car, find a second job, take out a loan, etc. etc. Place his mind on the merry-go-round of panic. Spend the next three days attaching fear to everything that is connected to money. Since you can't stop the check from arriving, you can torment the he*ven out of him in the meantime.

SINcerely,
SINister
CEO • PsyD, EdD

Day 6:
Wingless Planes

Gnash, today is a great day for creating further division in your partner's business relationships. You need to fine-tune the art of internal arguments. Your goal is to divide and separate, but again, it's not going to happen as you might think. You don't want him to stop being around other business partners, but instead, you want him to dissect every spoken word and create arguments in his head thus demonizing every partner he comes in to contact with.

In almost every conversation he's a part of, there will always be two sides or two camps much like there are in his little world of politics. So, we want to create a wingless plane within his mind. You don't want him to agree with the left or the right side, but instead, silently disagree with both sides so that eventually his mind crashes. You are the pilot in his ear.

Now, this doesn't mean that he's independent at all just because he's neither left or right. As you and I both know, independent is nonexistent as long as you are in the cockpit of his mind. Think about it. If you can confuse him and cause him to disagree with every statement that's spoken, then his tank will begin to fill with your most powerful fuel - pride!

Gnash, never forget or underestimate the power of pride. Just so you don't forget, I have strategically placed signage at fueling stations around your partner's business. Be on the lookout for Pacific Pride signs. These signs simply serve as reminders for you. Don't worry, your partner doesn't see these signs like we do because he's too inwardly focused on the lies that are now growing from your previous hard work.

xxx†xxx

Today's Tactic: Begin to encourage your partner to join a weekly religious business group. Be sure that this group shares the same religious beliefs that he aligns with. See if you can find a group that charges a monthly fee so that he shows up each week looking to receive something for his financial contribution. Also, don't discourage him from telling his co-workers about these weekly meetings. His sharing creates the perfect opportunity for hypocrisy to grow in the minds of his co-workers when they see him not using the tools he claims to get at his weekly meetings.

It's one thing for your partner to sit and listen to business talk in his work meetings all day long, but for him to sit and listen to business talk that's been infused with religion; this my friend is a theme park come true for you.

SINcerely,
SINister
CEO • PsyD, EdD

Day 7:
Online Steeples

Hello, Gnash. How fitting that we end the first week of emails on a Sunday. As you already know, today is a special day on your partner's calendar.

I'm going to give you every weapon I have in the category of church so that you will begin motivating your partner to only go to church online. I have multiple reasons for implementing this approach.

First, it's still too risky for your partner to have physical connection with anyone at the church building. If another partner were to either encourage him or pr*y with him, all of your work from the previous week could be gone with the wind.

Second, we want him to enj*y the comforts of his house. So, for the first part of the day once you have persuaded him to stay home, don't whisper one word to him. Leave him be. Let him bathe in this thing he refers to as pe*ce. While you will hate seeing him in this state, it's imperative that you give him a few hours of silence. You want him to think this pe*ce is a direct result of him staying home as opposed to going to the church building.

However, the moment you see that our planet has turned away from the sun, begin to softly whisper the tormenting thoughts about his Monday.

Then, begin to stretch out a new laundry list of lies from ear to ear about his boss. Then, rain down overwhelming thoughts about his ever-growing pile of bills that he can't seem to get out from under.

Lastly, for the rest of the night, pour on every tactic that you've learned this week. He will then start to wonder why Pe*ce left and if there was something he did that caused Pe*ce to leave. The moment he lies down to sleep, push over the first fearful domino of *What If?* As the dominos begin to fall, he will no longer be able to count sheep because all he will see is wolves. At this point, you can only h*pe that he will reach for his vice and begin to read work-related emails that keep him up late into the night. Remember, if he's worrying and emailing, he's not pr*ying or resting.

xxx†xxx

Today's Tactic: You know from studying your partner's case file the things he fears the most when it comes to what he thinks he bel*eves. So, any time he scrolls for a sermon or some silly spiritual podcast, do whatever you can to get him to listen to something related to a fearful topic. For some strange reason, your partner enj*ys listening to other partners talk about doing the things your partner is too scared to do. He is a weird creature this way.

As he is listening to one of these talks, remind him why he could never do what they are talking about. Tell him he's not cut out for it. Tell him he's not prepared. Tell him it's not his time. Tell him it's not his calling. Use his Book of lies against him. We can't stop him from being encouraged by what he hears other partners say, but we can torment him with fear during and after each little ~~pretend~~ pretentious podcast.

Don't worry, come Monday morning, the inspiring and motivational messages he listened to on Sunday, will be completely forgotten because of the tactics you have in store for him.

SINcerely,
SINister
CEO • PsyD, EdD

WEEK 2

Day 8:
Translation Separation

Gnash, here we go with Week 2! I h*pe you are excited about this week's timely tactics. It's important that we start this week with a little translation separation.

Since your partner is now attending a weekly religious business group, and going to church online, we need to add another layer of deception. One thing that is common in both his group and church is his leather-bound Book of lies. You need to introduce him to an online Book of lies because the online versions have over 1,900 translations. Imagine, if every partner in every group, online church, and podcast use a different translation, then separation will be inevitable. I've watched a plethora of partners divide from this tactic alone. There have even been cases where partners have completely abandoned their beliefs due to inconsistencies over these translations. Remember, sometimes it's the simple and small things they overlook that become our frog in the kettle.

I know what you might be thinking. I understand. While this Book of lies has the power to undo us, it's not the actual Book that does it. So, don't fear that he reads this Book.

But, if you are to fear, fear him eating his Book.

In the meantime, as he reads, point out the places where different translations contradict each other. You can start by whispering this all-time classic, "I wonder what this sentence says in the NIV?" If he switches translations, be ready to pounce. Then, plant doubt by whispering for him to try another translation. If then he abandons the App and begins to research the Greek for individual word origins, it's at this moment you'll know your whispered words are working. To take it to the next level, give him the idea to research trusted commentaries as well. I've noticed that commentaries have caused some partners to forget how to think. One last thing regarding commentaries. In his Book of lies, he is instructed to seek first the counsel of G*d. If he ends up always seeking first the counsel of commentaries, you win. We win. There's nothing better than when one partner seeks counsel from another partner first because we are the ones counseling each of them. Brilliant, huh?

xxx†xxx

Today's Tactic: Whisper the following words to your partner today, "What are the 16 omitted verses?" While this might seem like an ambiguous thing to say, he won't think anything odd about it because he's already questioning most of his thoughts now. What we are hoping to happen is that he Googles your question. When he does, he will find this on Wikipedia, *"The New Testament verses not included in modern English translations are verses of the New Testament that existed in older versions of the Bible (primarily the King James Version), but did not appear or were relegated to footnotes in later versions, such as the New International Version."* This article will definitely drop another straw on the camel's back of his beliefs. Lastly, tempt him to share this article with a partner that attends his religious business group. If he does, we will own that meeting!

SINcerely,
SINister
CEO • PsyD, EdD

Day 9:
The Stranger's Voice

Good morning, Gnash. Today's tactic is one of my least favorite tactics to inform you about, and so I'm not going to spend much time on it because of how much it angers me. This tactic is the epitome of gambling, but it must be discussed, and you'll soon see why.

There's a couple of sections in his Book of lies which instruct him to know your voice and not to follow your voice. If he finds this sentence or hears another partner quote it, you will have to work overtime on that day. Now, just because he reads this sentence, doesn't mean that he will actually understand it. That's our initial line of defense.

However, if you see him highlight this sentence, share this sentence, or Google anything about it, your time might be coming to an end. Be on guard.

The day he realizes that all of his thoughts aren't his own, is the day you could be reassigned.

So, how do you combat the effects of this sentence? The answer is twisted scripture. That's why I said this tactic is high-stakes gambling. It's at this point you will have to start whispering sentences out of context from his Book in h*pes that he uses these sentences in hatred as opposed to l*ve.

xxx†xxx

Today's Tactic: YouTube. We are huge fans of YouTube, not because of the videos but because of the vicious comments. See if you can get your partner to search "The stranger's voice". If he listens to you, the binge will begin. As he's watching these videos, give him the idea to start reading the comments. If he gets caught up crawling through the vertical web of meaningless comments, then there's a really high chance that he will start to bel*eve more in the voices of mental health than his Book of lies. I know what you are going to say, but he doesn't know that mental health is our covert umbrella company.

It's incredibly insane how partners refer to YouTube comments as the gutter of the internet, yet they continue to return to them as the dog Bathsheba's son referred to in Pr*verbs.

SINcerely,
SINister
CEO • PsyD, EdD

Day 10:
Predictable M.O.

Good morning, Gnash! Today we are going to be focusing on the areas where your partner is predictable in his mode of operation. You're going to want to hang a *Do Not Disturb* sign on your partners ear if he falls into anything routine. We l*ve routine. We l*ve plain, passive, and ponds. We l*ve the same old vanilla, the same chair, the same shows, the same restaurant, and the same route to work because same is not sane.

Routine will allow you to autopilot your tactics which gives you time to plan darker ploys. Also, our data shows, the longer a partner soaks in the pool of routine, the less likely he will respond to anything new. Remember, his Book of lies constantly uses the word *Go*. We loathe these two letters.

Your partner is no threat to us when he's in the middle of a stagnate routine. In fact, next time you find him sitting in his same old chair, watching the same show on the same weeknight, whisper, "Be still and know that I am G*d." When you can tell that he enj*yed those words, give him a moment to calmly exhale and then immediately blast him with, "Go ye therefore and make disciples." The moment you see a negative facial reaction, follow up with, "Why do I continue to do the same thing day after day?" Now, this will cause him to sit there confused, condemned, and less likely to do anything at all which will keep him in the quicksand of routine.

xxx†xxx

Today's Tactic: Trick your partner to bel*eve that Saturday is his personal day. Get him in a routine of thinking and living this way. Give him productive ideas so that he feels like he is checking things off an important list. Do this each and every Saturday. The more we can get him to focus on himself and his little corner of the world, the more we can condemn him on Sunday.

SINcerely,
SINister
CEO • PsyD, EdD

Day 11:
The Feeding of the Followers

Gnash, I h*pe all is delightfully dark in your corner of the world. Today, you will be implementing an epic tactic that your partner will never see coming. Because you are doing everything you can to keep him on the socialpathic path, you can now begin to implement a new selfish strategy.

You are going to make him think he's having kingdom impact by causing him to focus his on his number of followers. Yes, he subscribes to the sentence from his Book of lies that he is to be the follower, but as soon as he gets a taste of being followed, he won't be able to stop focusing on his fake flock. By the way, we don't care who he follows or who follows him; we only care about the numbers.

Constantly bombard him with thoughts regarding his fluctuating number of followers. Cause him to obsess over his subscribers, likes, and comments. He must come to a point where these narcissistic numbers validate who he is so that when the platforms fade, his identity does as well. You can't forget how fragile he is most of the time. He lives in a world where almost every posted word is heavily scrutinized. Much like his blood pressure, we desire to increase the number when it comes to offending partners. This keeps him in a constant state of worry while second-guessing the words he so carefully chooses.

Anytime his numbers dip from a lost subscriber or follower, aggressively attack him with thoughts of being a bad witness or false prophet. But, then, immediately after attacking him, encourage him to add an addendum to his post, clarifying what he was trying to say. Many of his followers will then question what they previously thought before he clarified what he originally was trying to say. This should create a carousel on confusion and comments that spin round and round thus causing your partner to check his numbers even more. Lastly, do not tempt him to hide the post that created the collapse, because you'll want to work this post together for bad at a later date.

xxx†xxx

Today's Tactic: On the days where your partner is lounging in routine, use this time to create a strategy of lies that he can use for quickly growing his subscriber base. As you might know, the more subscribers he has, the more money he makes. If he begins to make more money because of his followers, you can then tempt him to quit his job, and he can "Jerry Maguire" his boss. You and I both know that his job is secure and that his make-bel*eve land of likes is not, but you can get him to see it differently. If you can deceive him into quitting his job, you'll have more opportunities to chop at the root of his fa*th while he travels to the land he knows not of. Our goal in all of this is for him to focus on self, deny the challenge, and follow your voice.

SINcerely,
SINister
CEO • PsyD, EdD

Day 12:
Isolation Kingdom

Good morning, %%First Name%%. Today's strategy has to be thinly sliced and stacked over time at a sloth's pace. You need to make sure your partner doesn't get too connected with other partners. Only you know his level of connections. I'm not so much concerned with superficial or deep relationships as much as I am with the frequency of connections.

As you know, we have lost many of the lost due to the magnetization of what they refer to as unconditional l*ve. Their ability to quickly create ties with one another is something we've still yet to figure out.

Also, know that some of their strongest ties form in moments of chaos, tragedy, and loss. That's why you can never push too hard when you whisper thoughts. All of this being said, we gain the most ground and make the biggest impact when partners are marinating in isolation. While they do have the ability to be bulletproof in isolation, most are not equipped nor know how to handle this type of environment. Again, that's why so many of them turn quickly to each other first. So, you need to be creating crafty words that cause him to isolate from all partners both good and bad.

A few types of isolation which have worked in the past are getaways, inner closets, daily devotions, and even the result of poor weather.

Now, here's the flip side to the list above. If at any time you see your partner putting into practice the things he's learning in these places, discontinue the whispers that encourage him to retreat. However, if he is using these retreats as excuses to be alone, then his chase lounge is your battlefield. So, take a knee, and camp out right beside him. Follow along with what he's reading, and counter. If you see him switch from taking notes to picking up his Book of lies, tell him that he might need to check his phone to see if any partner has tried to reach him. H*pefully, this will distract him.

Remember, don't push too hard in these environments because we don't want him to ever trade his alone time for meeting with other partners. Keep in mind, where one or less is gathered with our thoughts, isolation reigns.

xxx†xxx

Today's Tactic: If your partner takes the bait and quits his job to become a self-proclaimed online socio-guru, then you will have to convince him to operate his digital empire from his little four-walled kingdom. We want him to play solitary in solitary confinement. We want him to slowly lose all social skills due to being in isolation. We want him to think he's being wise by not spending money on commuting. We want him to light candles, play music, brew coffee, and drift away in lonely comfort. Why? Because bearded infants who lack courage never leave the house. His crib-like kingdom is the only setting that rivals the womb. This strategy of isolation mixed with any previous tactic becomes a deadly cocktail for tormenting your partner.

SINcerely,
SINister
CEO • PsyD, EdD

Day 13:
Seek 1st 501c3

Good afternoon, Gnash. I noticed the last email we sent out, once again had errors with the First Name field. We are h*ping to upgrade from our Windows NT system in the near future. This would remedy the problem.

Today's sly strategy is another way you can glide underneath the radar of your partner's awareness. As you already know, your partner gives a pre-defined percentage to a couple of nonprofits each month. Note: We do not want to stop him from giving. In fact, we'd like for him to give more, but not monetarily. I want you to guilt him into giving more by telling him to volunteer time that he doesn't have. If you can make him feel obscenely obligated to go above and beyond because it's such a great cause, he will then grow more tired and weary. When he grows tired and weary, you will have greater access to his emotions.

As you are working this angle, be sure to also continually drip stats down his ear canal about how important the 501c3 is to their kingdom. But, only do so with his nonprofit of choice. Make him think that his nonprofit is more important than all of the other nonprofits. We want to slowly transform him into a single purpose crusader so that he looks down on all other nonprofits. There's nothing more confusing to partners when they see another partner who is both prideful and philanthropic at the same time.

If you can accomplish this while wearing him down through volunteering, you will string together a consecutive number of victories. Don't lose sight of the mission. We aren't trying to kill him. We are trying to torment him as much as possible, and we do this with thoughts. Everything we do starts and ends with thoughts.

The thoughts around nonprofits,

giving, volunteering, and obligation all work together with your other strategies. You must constantly be tweaking your words so that he lives a l*fe of mental *Whack-A-Mole*.

xxx†xxx

Today's Tactic: Tell your partner to buy a couple of tables for the next life-changing event. We don't care about how much money the nonprofit raises or how many partners arrive at their dumb little dinner.

As your partner begins to invite other partners with the use of texts, emails, and letters, attack him every time he clicks send. Begin to build grudges in his mind regarding the partners who haven't replied. Speak lies about each and every soul on his invitation list. Then, pour on the anxiety about the tables that haven't been filled as the circled date nears. If everything goes as planned, he will be a mental mess on the big night and you will be the one who profits with his nonprofit.

Lastly, to add more fuel to his ever-growing fire of guilt, plant the following idea in his mind. Tell him if he makes an enormously high bid on an auction item, that he can profit in three ways. A.) He will look super generous to all the other partners, B.) He will get a tax write-off for his donation, and C.) He can have a friend sell his item for him on Craigslist to recoup some of the money he lost. This three-headed plan will surely pique his interest.

SINcerely,
SINister
CEO • PsyD, EdD

Day 14:
David's Deception

Gnash, welcome to the end of Week 2. I h*pe you are starting to see some cognitive cancer spread throughout your partners mind. Usually, by the end of Week 2, we see a 50% increase in fear, guilt, anxiety, depression, and shame.

Today's special is a delightful dish of deception that's been garnished with three pinches of denial and comes with a side of organic betrayal. If you look at the attached photos, you will see a few of the past partners who have tasted this dish, including David, Peter, and Judas.

For now, I want to focus your attention on the David portion of the dish. Your partner looks up to this little runt he calls King David. He tends to focus on the tragic Goliath victory, the lucky cave moment, and all of the sappy Psalms that David wrote. However, your partner has somehow never heard the beautiful story about Uriah. So, you are going to recreate this story in your partner's l*fe.

As you know, your partner tends to focus on a particular part of a woman. He does this because of the words that were whispered to him in his youth. Every time your partner walks past that particular married female partner at his work, whisper into his eyes. We want him to eventually go beyond just looking. Now, don't get ahead of me and think this strategy is about sex. It's not. Sex is just one of the tools we use to create torment and death.

When it comes time for your partner to make his deceptive move, it would be ideal if you could time your words for when she's ovulating and then push him over the edge of temptation. (FYI: Regarding that one sentence from his Book of lies, he doesn't bel*eve he will be provided a way out of this type of temptation. Plus, even if the way is provided, you will flood his mind so he only sees the path of curves.)

Now, here's part two of the plan. You must get him to impregnate and abandon her immediately. This will leave her in a vulnerable and insecure state so that she feels forced to abort the little unformed partner. Then after the abortion takes place, h*pefully, she will live a long and tormented l*fe of guilt and shame. Later, when you tell your partner about all the chaos he has caused her, you can then show him in his quiet time how he's just like his hero, David.

xxx†xxx

Today's Tactic: Before you introduce the Bathsheba plan to your partner, first have your partner make friends with her husband. I think you see where I'm going with this. If your partner is able to see her at his friend's house while going to hang out with him, then over time, nobody will have malicious thoughts about your partner being at her house. Once your partner has established trust and loyalty with his friend, then you can light the fuse on the Bathsheba plan. I can't wait to get an update on this masterful plan!

SINcerely,
SINister
CEO • PsyD, EdD

WEEK 3

Day 15:
Wounded Birds & Words

Gnash, here's to a new week of more tormenting! Today's strategy can be used at any time, but also implement immediately if the scheme for the female at his work falls apart. You should know, today's strategy works more than nine times out of ten on female partners.

Also, I'm assuming that you have finished reading The Official CIA Manual of Trickery and Deception by H. Keith Melton and Robert Wallace since it was on your required reading list. Remember, you must constantly be acquiring more knowledge while your partner sleeps. The more tools you have, the further you can stay ahead of him.

Regarding this female partner at his work, she is referred to in our kingdom as a *Wounded Bird*. Your partner sees her as a sweet, soft, and sexy individual. However, you need to cause him to look beneath the outward and see where she's inwardly wounded so that he can see her weakness in order to obtain her flesh. He needs to see her as prey. She is not to be respected or seen as a specimen to marry or l*ve.

There are two ways for your partner to accomplish this goal that you need not take lightly. He has to be delicate, and unfortunately, pati*nt.

Also, tell him to hang on every word she says while she's talking. Most of the time we don't want partners to listen to each other, but in this case, listening is the key to opening her guarded place of brokenness. Make sure you do not distract him while he's listening but do whisper questions for the answers you need to know. Because of her outward beauty, most male partners don't hear a word she says. You and he both need every word she speaks, so be sure to tell him to keep eye contact. Once you discover where she was wounded, break out your poetic playbook of responses and begin to reel her in. If all goes according to plan, your partner will own her affections in less than three weeks. Even if you see an opportunity for him to pounce early, don't let him. We don't want her to detect anything that could remind her of the past. As you have learned, time creates trust. And, trust creates the one night we need to take place.

xxx†xxx

Today's Tactic: Most of the time, a female's significant other becomes routinely comfortable and secure in his relationship after two or three months. They are now beyond this point. This means she's receiving less daily affirmations from him than she was in the beginning when they were saturated with infatuation. This is good news and yet another key to guaranteeing your partner's success.

Be sure to amply equip him the soothing words she longs to hear. Have him write these words on little notes and leave them in strategic places on her desk. Make sure he doesn't write anything that could be taken sexually but only use words that mend the places where she has been cut so deeply. At the very moment you smell codependency emanating from her he*rt, your partner must begin to gently infuse the word l*ve into his language. It will only be a matter of hours after the spoken lie of l*ve, when, for the first time, you will see two doves killed with one word.

SINcerely,
SINister
CEO • PsyD, EdD

Day 16:
The Worries of What If?

Good evening, Gnash. We purposely sent this message tonight as opposed to our previously scheduled time in the morning. Why? We thought it would be a great segway into today's topic of *What If*.

As you probably have already noticed with your partner, he doesn't truly trust or have fa*th in the things he proclaims. He comes across strong and courageous to other partners, but you see him when he's alone. You see how he lives in a constant state of worry. You hear how often he says, "Well, what if?…"

While his partners don't hear the fear behind the *What If* question, you can see it draped all over his body language. Let's capitalize on this question of fear. Now that you have bombarded him with two weeks' worth of tormenting tactics, it's time to fire off a series of targeted *What Ifs* to each little location where he houses fear. You might be thinking, "What if he counters my *What Ifs*?" The only way he can truly counter is if he seeks first the counsel of his G*d. But, I'm trusting that you've drastically minimized that approach over the last two weeks.

Also, if he audibly quotes scripture or squawks any of his battle songs, you have counter-attack weapons for those as well. Remember, just because he sings, "This is how I fight my battles", doesn't mean that he's fighting his battles. He might just be proclaiming the method about how he would fight his battles. Big difference. Pay attention to the details.

Another battle cry he likes to stutter is, "For the weapons of our warfare are not carnal but mighty in blah blah blah." He thinks he bel*eves this sentence, but he doesn't know what the weapons are, because his sentence only says what the weapons are not. Even if he did know, it wouldn't stop you from dropping your *What If* grenades every time he said it or read it. Until he finds the one way to defeat you, know that your ammo will always work.

xxx†xxx

Today's Tactic: Tonight, while your partner sleeps, go through his Book of lies and highlight every place where his G*d promises to do something for His partners. Then, begin to memorize these pathetic promises. Memorizing these sentences will give you a war chest of *What Ifs* to detonate when you hear your partner proclaim or sing these promises. I'll give you a few examples.

Your partner says • You say:
"The L*rd will fight for you!"
But, What If He doesn't?

"He gives strength to the weary."
But, What If I continue to mess up?

"So, do not fear for I am with you."
But, What If I can't tell that You are?

"No weapon forged against you will prevail."
But, What If I use the weapon on myself?

"If any of you lacks wisdom, you should ask G*d, who gives generously to all without finding fault, and it will be given to you."
But, What If I don't take it because I'm too dumb to see it?

SINcerely,
SINister
CEO • PsyD, EdD

Day 17:
Gambling for 65 at 25

Good morning, Gnash. Today's strategy is going to be quite risky. It's important that you know there's a fine line we have to walk when it comes to the conversation about money.

For some partners, money creates a false feeling somewhere between happiness and j*y, while for others, money doesn't even move their narcissistic needle.

It appears as if each partner is quite unique when it comes to chasing after money, so you will have to tiptoe through the money waters of his mind to learn where he stands. If he's in the minority of partners that prefer time over money, you will need to roll out Plan A (see attachment). But, if he's like most partners, the majority of his thoughts will be consumed with consumerism, so you will need to implement Plan B (see attachment). Here's how you can find out which plan best suits your partner. Even though your partner is only 25 years old, you should start to whisper thoughts about planning for the future. Use terms such as savings, 401k, stocks, bonds, and my retirement. Be sure to use the word my in front of retirement; that wasn't a typo. Why? Because we never want any partner to save for someone else's retirement. You must use only words that pertain to him and his special life only.

Now, if you see him start to head down the mental path of retirement where he actually starts saving and investing, you must then begin to drip more fear regarding the fluctuations of his money on an ongoing basis.

On the other side of the coin, if he begins making strides to protect his time so that he can invest it in other things, you'll want to interrupt that as well. At the end of the day, like they so often say, we don't want him to possess any margin at any time, in any category of l*fe. Don't spend too much time worrying about it though. You have plenty of tactics to deceive him with either way. See, with too much money, you can cause him to fear losing it all while making him feel guilty for working so much. With too much margin, you can have more time to make him feel guilty for not working more and investing. This is why we own the spiritual world when it comes to mammon.

xxx†xxx

Today's Tactic: No matter which path your partner strolls down, he will need some amount of money for all of l*fe's journeys. So, you need to pave both paths with doubt and post sad signs that scream third-world guilt. Tempt him non-stop with *Buy Now* and then upon checkout make him feel like a selfish miser. After that, be sure to closely track his thoughts while he's tracking his package so you can make sure he's solely focused on himself.

SINcerely,
SINister
CEO • PsyD, EdD

Day 18:
Millstone Madness

Good morning, Gnash. While your partner does not have any offspring, you need to plan now for when these tiny sphinx-like gremlins arrive. Partner offspring have the ability to grow a unique type of l*ve within your subject that will make your career much more difficult than it has to be. On the flip side, if your skills are dialed in by the time his gremlins hatch, you could use the hatchlings against him and vice-versa.

When the time comes, one of the best ways to separate your partner from his hatchling is through your partner's ego. You can accomplish this by planting certain thoughts about his career. You want your partner to think the only way to impact other partners is by traveling all over the globe. Also, speak thoughts about accumulating more education and acronyms so that his spare time will have to be allocated towards higher learning. The less time your partner spends with his hatchling, the more impact you can make with the hatchling. One day, we will devise a plan to make sure the hatchling bel*eves that your partner chose fame and fortune over fam*ly.

Now, the third option, which is actually our first option, starts with your partner's spouse. From the very day she conceives, we will feed her an assembly line of thoughts about abortion. We want her to wisely make the biggest and best decision of her l*fe. If she chooses to end it before it begins, then you can proceed with the painful rounds of depression on him.

Words cannot express how much we enj*y seeing generations and destinies evaporate due to one little decision being made. Imagine being able to pile on previous tactics at the same time your partner is going through an unbearable amount of pain and sorrow. This is a moment we live for and you should aspire to as well.

xxx†xxx

Today's Tactic: If in the case your partner doesn't fall for or follow the business travel path once the hatchling arrives, there's another tactic we've recently discovered in this past decade called, *The iSolate*. As you might have noticed, almost every partner walks around staring at a small vibrant vice. This vice has been known to render some partners completely useless which gives you more one-on-one time with your partner. So, if you can get your partner to bury his face in his vice, especially when partners are talking to him, you can create many dark chasms. Then, one day, when the hatchlings arrive, and he's now addicted to his vice, they won't ever know what undivided attention feels or looks like.

SINcerely,
SINister
CEO • PsyD, EdD

Day 19:
Calendar Saturation

Gnash, I can't wait to read your replies after this campaign ends. I trust because you are reading these emails, you're putting each one into practice.

Today's strategy is all about theft by receiving through the use of your partner's calendar. As you know, your partner has a hard time saying no. He's completely spineless whenever other partners ask him to do something or volunteer for their cause. The reason why is because he never developed the no-muscle when he was young. We deceived his parents on a daily basis so that they wouldn't have the temerity to teach him how to do so.

Because of his innocuous behavior, he ends up being tossed like a wave to and fro from one commitment to another. It's cute how he tells himself that he's being a servant. He doesn't realize he's actually a shackled slave behind the bars of his calendar. This lousy trait is an excellent quality because you can leverage his weakness eight days a week.

First, repeatedly tell him that he has a servant's h*art because it will cause an abscess of false humility to fester.

Second, you need him to be running from one place to another at all times so you can cater his cranium party with cortisol cocktails.

Lastly, you want your partner to buckle under the pressure and become paralyzed when he sees all things packed into his calendar.

Over time, this will wear him down, and he will become both emotionally and physically sick. This state of sickness is where our spiral begins, and it's here that you will get to try tactics that he's previously tasted and rejected.

xxx † xxx

Today's Tactic: It's super important that you completely confuse and deceive your partner with this calendar concept.

So, you need to keep an eye out for the most sensitive and passionate female partner that he knows who also runs a nonprofit. When she inevitably invites your partner to her life-or-death event, begin the persuasive whisper for him to exercise his no-muscle. Here's why.

The moment he says no, and then sees the genuine look of sadness on her face, he will never want to say no again. We need her pudgy little face burned into his memory whenever he thinks about using the word no. This imagery of her face will cause him to be both torn and tormented at the same time.

Gnash! Do not let up on him. Consistency is your silent companion.

Think about it; if over a ten or twenty year period you can smear shame across the landscape of his mind by simply getting him to use one two-letter word, how priceless would that be?

SINcerely,
SINister
CEO • PsyD, EdD

Day 20:
Divine Wine

Good morning, Gnash! Today is a day to celebrate. So, grab a crystal goblet, and let's pour a fifth of shame into your partner's mind. In case you didn't know, there are two diametrically opposed camps in his congregation when it comes to the topic of wine.

However, we don't care about either camp. In all of history, alcohol has never been the problem, even though we have deceived them into thinking this way. The fact that they divide over liquid is hilariously ludicrous to me. As for your partner, he's still confused on which camp to join because he sees both sides of the argument.

This is where you slide in. It's time I introduce you to the third camp where the embers of deception never burn out. You don't want him to abstain nor do you want him to drink every night. What you want is for him to taste the lukewarm l*fe of both camps. Moving forward, find exciting ways to tempt him with just one glass, so you can then push him over the edge into the entire bottle.

Then, when you tempt him to quit drinking, you can cause him to judge others who are drinking. When he decides to return to drinking, but only in moderation, you will then fuel his fire with the dry logs of hypocrisy. When he feels like a hypocrite and doesn't know what to do, point him to sentences in His book of lies where j*sus drank at parties.

Then, you can invite justification to the party. Once justification arrives at the party, condemnation will soon walk through the door to party as well. After condemnation hangs out for a bit, your partner will soon cave and order another drink. Finally, you can then copy and paste this cycle of chaos over and over again throughout his days.

Please, don't forget, while doing all of this, you must keep him mentally in the middle. You want him on the wall that divides the two camps, only hopping off now and then to travel back and forth. He must never stay in one camp. He must live in the lukewarm land of lies, and sleep on the wall made of chaos, confusion, and deception. We made the wall. We own the wall. The wall is the place where tormenting never ends.

It's now time you start to double-dip. If you take the following tactic and mix it with the previous calendar tactic, you might gain ground quicker. However, you must be careful not to push too hard because you want him engulfed in torment, but not on the brink of suicide. We never want any partner to commit suicide. While suicide does cause fam*lies to mourn - which we enj*y, your goal is to torment your partner for a l*fetime, not for a short time.

xxx†xxx

Today's Tactic: We strongly desire to see partners become members of anonymous groups where they never experience true mental freedom. While we do run the risk of relationships forming at these meetups, it's worth the trade-off when we get a partner to bel*eve he's chained even though he's free. So, begin to coerce your partner into joining one group or five groups since his calendar is already completely crammed. Tell him without community and accountability; he doesn't stand a chance, because his G*d only helps those who help themselves.

Remember, our DUI is getting him to make decisions under the influence of tormenting.

SINcerely,
SINister
CEO • PsyD, EdD

Day 21:
5-Hour Sloth

Gnash! Good morning to you. I h*pe you are reading this during the early part of the morning in preparation for your pathetic partner's day.

As a reminder, we don't sleep in. Partners sleep in. However, there are some partners who climb out of bed at dawn to spend time in pr*yer. If your partner is one of the few who performs this pointless act, you must end it immediately. I only say it's pointless because we don't see the effects of his ramblings. Yet, there's something uncomfortable that we feel when we see it happening. I know. It's confusing. As of now, make all other tactics secondary to this one.

So, here's how you counter-attack. Once you slowly and methodically slide Sloth into the picture, Laziness will follow. At the same time, you must also whisper little tweets about the power that sleep holds. But, you must only encourage sleep in the morning, and never at night. You want him to stay in bed, but not to sleep. You want him to toss and turn under the sheets of torment while thinking about the heaviness of his day. If you succeed, Anxiety will follow him throughout the day. You want this to happen because Anxiety is the child of torment that breeds Exhaustion. Exhaustion is like sickness; he creates holes in the wall where you can gain easier access to the depths of your partner's mind. You are the Trojan Horse, and your words are the soldiers that infiltrate his mind. It all starts with Sloth.

Now, tonight, I want you to cross over the drawbridge and release the legion of slothful thoughts while he sleeps. The city is yours.

xxx†xxx

Today's Tactic: One of the greatest strategies to use while the foundation of sloth dries, is procrastination. Here's why. Your partner, unfortunately, was originally equipped with the ability to create. I gotta be honest with you, there's not much he can't do. This should be alarming to you. However, if you can get him to procrastinate every time he gets an idea from the inferior kingdom, then you can keep his creativity on pause while you implement other tormenting tactics.

Also, keep your ears tuned for whenever he uses the word *decided*. If procrastination hasn't fully matured, the byproduct of *decided* could be your kryptonite. Partners are always deciding things, and while most never do anything after making a decision, it only takes a dozen bel*evers to change our world.

SINcerely,
SINister
CEO • PsyD, EdD

WEEK 4

Day 22:
Just & Yeah, But!

Gnash, you are really going to enj*y today's email because this strategy is probably the easiest one to embed. It's taken centuries for us to fine-tune this strategy, but we've finally mastered it. I won't say it works on every partner, but the numbers do speak for themselves.

As you know, while we do have many tactics, we only have one weapon. Our weapon has always been, and will always be our whisper.

Of course, they can never know this secret because we rely on partners to simply listen and carry out our commands. That being said, today we are going to talk about the twisting of words. We want your partner to go along thinking that society's bad words are the bad words not to say;

while continuing to use the l*fe-decaying words he unknowingly uses day in and day out.

You are probably too young to know this, but decades ago we planted a few choice phrases they are still using today. Such classics include: *Bite Your Tongue. If You Can't Say Something Nice, Don't Say Anything At All. No Comment.* and *Say You're Sorry!*

To this day, partners are still clueless about what these phrases aren't addressing. So, until they wake from their verbal coma, we will keep cursing them with the unknown curse words they use.

xxx†xxx

Today's Tactic: Effective tomorrow, you are to begin cursing your partner with the phrases *Yeah, But!* and *Just.* These two prefaces have a way of causing ongoing doubt and insecurity without your partner knowing it. Trust me, your partner could use a heavy dose of each.

First, regarding *Yeah, But!*, you need to exercise this phrase whenever anyone reads or quotes a sentence from his Book of lies. You want him to doubt this Book and its validity. If over time, he ends up viewing this Book as a collection of contradictions, then he's yours!

Second, regarding *Just*, you need to insert this word before any noun he uses to describe himself. If done correctly, your partner will end up sounding like that dramatically depressed donkey that slothfully mopes around with his half-naked, yellow bear friend.

SINcerely,
SINister
CEO • PsyD, EdD

Day 23:
Conference Constipation

Good morning, Gnash. "Today's email is brought to you by this year's gold sponsors. If it wasn't for their generous donations, these emails wouldn't be possible." How many times have you heard this type of statement?

Is your partner attending this week's conference? And, what about the conference the following week? If not, he must. We want partners to consistently attend conferences while juggling everything else in their lives because this brings burnout. We want them to consume a steady diet of conferences while remaining mentally constipated. We want them to take scores of notes, so we can shame them for not applying the principles. We want them to donate funds, so we can make them feel guilty for not giving more.

Again, while we do run the risk of partners creating relationships with other partners at these conferences, our data shows this doesn't happen enough to offset the collateral damage we cause at conferences. Also, this might come as a shock to you, but we want your partner to gain more knowledge. We want him always learning something new at each conference he attends. However, we never want him to do anything with the knowledge. If you can keep his mind in a deceived state of being overwhelmed, you won't have to worry about application.

I'm still surprised that most partners haven't picked up on our strategy, especially the partners who were once 4-year college students. Let me explain. Notice I said 4-year, not 20-year college students. In the land of higher learning, there comes a point when partners move from learning to application. Yet, with conference junkies, they just continue to hoard information year after year. So, you must continue to find ways for your partner to do the same. We want him to be his own self-storage unit. We want his unit to become so full, that he has to rent another unit.

Metaphorically speaking, you want every square inch of his unit to be filled with knowledge on how to lose weight, along with housing the pricey treadmills that have never been used. Then, when he's at his next nonprofit conference and the over-paid Asker begins talking about investing in the lives of partners as opposed to buying material things, you can immediately start to shame him with images of his dust-covered treadmills. Following that, you can remind him how he's never lost any weight, and then begin listing off the number of calories that are piled on his hundred-dollar plate.

Next, whisper encouraging thoughts of deflection so that he begins to judge the partners at his table who defile their temple more than he does. Oh!

Do all of this while the keynote clown is pr*ying for the less fortunate so that your partner doesn't hear a single word that's being said. Lastly, the moment the pr*yer ends, tell your partner to quickly access his checking account balance on his vice to see if he has enough money to buy a bottle of wine on the way home. Once he gets home and begins to drink, you can then remind him of the things he learned at the conference now that he's too tired and intoxicated to do anything. Cheers!

xxx†xxx

Today's Tactic: Tonight, while your partner sleeps, comb through his pile of notes from the past year's conferences. Be on the lookout for his personal highlights. Memorize each highlighted line. Look for common themes in his notes from each conference. You will begin to notice an alarming pattern. His

G*d is trying to weave a tapestry of thoughts from these highlights in order to reveal the plans He has for your partner. His G*d somehow finds a way to take all the errors we cause and turn them into good. It's disgusting. You must unravel His lame strategy. If your partner discovers what his G*d is trying to tell him, all of your tactics will slowly begin to die like the leaves in ~~the~~ Fall. Then, over time, you would be left with only one last tactic, which I will discuss in the final email.

SINcerely,
SINister
CEO • PsyD, EdD

Day 24:
PG-13 Rules!

Gnash, I h*pe you're having a child-like morning because today we are going back to the dark and decaying halls of elementary.

Here's why. Long ago, we unfortunately lost one of our greatest partners due to a blinding incident on a certain road I will not mention. After this man became lost, he began to combat our efforts by sending letters to other goats. He once said, "You have been beli*vers so long now that you ought to be teaching others. Instead, you need someone to teach you again the basic things about G*d's word. You are like babies who need milk and cannot eat solid food." Isn't that statement amazing? These babies needed to be taught again because of the curriculum we instituted.

As you can see, I'm full of pride regarding this acknowledgment he unknowingly gave us.

So, let's talk about a bold strategy to demote your partner back to breast feeding. In 1968, a traitor inside of the MPAA rolled out the Rated R stamp to help partners decide what films were inappropriate for their offspring. This was not a good year for us. It took us 16 years to recover, conceive, and give birth to a new strategy. But then, on July 1, 1984, we quietly countered, and once again, the teachers became babies. We gave our strategy the code name PG-13 for *Partners Get Triskaidekaphobia*. Of course, the partners had no clue what it stood for at the time.

See, your partner has chosen not to watch Rated R movies unless, of course, he can justify it due to a war setting or real-l*fe events - he's become quite skilled in the department of justification (Good job!). So, don't waste your time on tempting him to watch Rated R movies. In fact, no need for temptation at all when it comes to these movies. Your strategy is to simply and calmly suggest a wide assortment of PG-13 movies that he might enj*y watching. That's it. This is another category where you can kill two doves with one bullet. I'll explain. One, if he's watching a 2-hour movie, guess what he's not doing? In this time slot, he's not living his l*fe of highlights that we previously discussed. Two, while he thinks he's watching something "safe" because of its PG-13 rating, our pre-programmed messages are attacking his other immune system. Our PG-13 strategy has been in place now for over 35 years and somehow most partners continue to think these ratings are about age. Every morning, I wake up shocked to see so many milk-sipping partners still blindly conforming to the ways of our whispers.

xxx†xxx

Today's Tactic: Another great year for us was 2007 because it was the year that partners were no longer limited to watching their favorite series just once a week. When we released this strategy, we knew that partners would lose their minds. Our data showed us that if we were to let partners demand back-to-back episodes, inside a digital library of endless categories for a nominal monthly fee, while remaining isolated from other partners, that we would be able to immobilize the masses. We bel*eved that if we could stream thoughts hour after hour, day after day as opposed to just once a week, that Sloth would eventually give birth to something in which no century in history has ever seen. And, she did. We now have baby Binge in a PG-13 world of *Watch Again* and *Recommended for You*. Roll credits.

SINcerely,
SINister
CEO • PsyD, EdD

Day 25:
Little Black Truths

Good morning, %%First Name%%. I've been looking forward to sending you today's email for awhile. The closer we get towards the end, the more deceptive we have to be with our strategies. So, here we go.

I'm sure you're familiar with a phrase your partner uses called *Little White Lies*. Don't get me wrong, while it's great that he's telling lies; I don't like that he's aware of it. Over the centuries, we have tried to shame partners when they say a little white lie, but it doesn't work because they justify it so quickly. Because of their justification, we've had to devise a new plan. We are currently calling this new strategy *Little Black Truths*.

Here's how it works. This week, whenever your partner visits his religious business group, goes to church, or attends a conference, you must quickly whisper context and culture about his Book of lies the moment another partner quotes a sentence from their Book of lies. He needs to get caught up playing a spiritual game of *Whack-A-Mole* with these sentences so that pride takes root in his mind.

This strategy might sound a bit confusing, so I'll give you a few examples. Let's pretend he's at his religious business group, and the conversation around the table is about church attendance. If one of the partners say, "Well, you know br*ther, we are not to forsake the gathering blah blah blah." Immediately, you whisper to your partner, "Actually, that sentence is talking about persecution, not attendance."

Now, it doesn't matter which partner is correct. We don't care. What matters is that we got Bitterness and Division to have a seat at the table.

xxx†xxx

Today's Tactic: This week your partner will probably attend church with his f*mily. As usual, I still want you to whisper words of entitlement during worship, and cause distraction during the message, but wait until the very moment everyone gets in the car to go home before you use this tactic. The very moment the last car door shuts, get your partner to ask, "What did y'all think of church today?". This question always stirs up dissension and negativity, which in turn gives us more ammo for each partner in the future. We want the crows to fly through the sunroof and grab the seeds before the rain comes.

SINcerely,
SINister
CEO • PsyD, EdD

Day 26:
Hooked on Phoneics

%%First Name%%, we regret to tell you our email client came down with the worm virus. Our IT department is looking into the problem. We h*pe to have your name corrected in time for the next email. Please know, you are very important to us, %%First Name%%.

While we briefly addressed the following strategy in a previous email, today we are going to dive a bit deeper into the world of *Hooked on Phoneics*. It goes without mentioning that our mobile D-vice strategy has been quite the success. While there are a fraction of partners who have exercised the disc*pline to both limit their usage and do great things with their D-vice, the high majority of partners have fallen into our trap. There was a time when partners said idle hands are our playground, but we've switched the game since then. While they were busying finding things to do so they wouldn't be idle, we placed a D-vice in their hands.

Now, you must find deceptive ways for your partner to never be hands-free. He must carry his D-vice everywhere he goes. He must eat with it, shower with it, pr*y with it, and even go to bed with it. Over time, we want his D-vice to be the only omnipresent thing in his l*fe.

One way that you can accomplish this strategy is by charging his D-vice with fear. Because your partner feels irrelevant and alone, even though he's proud of being digitally connected across the globe, you must torment him with meaningless notifications. And, when the notifications have ceased, and he still checks his D-vice anyway, remind him how nobody cares about him. Tell him he doesn't matter. Tell him to give up. Then, tempt him to troll through other people's pictures, so that you can inject him with comparison every time he sees someone who has something he doesn't have. Don't worry; you can't push too hard when it comes to his D-vice. It's too late. It's already become a part of him. He can't leave it behind. He can't be without it. Yet, he doesn't see it as a problem because we equipped it with the knowledge of good and great.

xxx†xxx

Today's Tactic: It's time to add a new layer of narcissism to your partner's mental Home Screen.

Since all partners get uglier and older each day, tempt your partner to take selfies so you can remind him how he doesn't measure up.

Since he's so full of himself, after he chooses the best photo of his face from the twenty photos he took, have him seek the approval of other partners by posting it on face-book. Don't worry about the engagements because Likes and comments are like fireworks - they only last for a brief moment. Lastly, as he smiles about each little red he*rt, begin to pop them with tormenting thoughts about tomorrow.

SINcerely,
SINister
CEO • PsyD, EdD

Day 27:
Jim & Jen Gym

Good morning, %%First Name%%. Today's strategy fits nicely next to yesterday's strategy. The goal over the next few weeks is to capitalize on your partner's flaws by encouraging him to become a member of the local fitness club. Tell him he should join for health-related reasons, and later you can slowly feed his narcissism with tactics I will be discussing in this email.

At the end of the day (which you know doesn't apply to us), we don't care about good health or hot bodies, bad health or chubby bodies. The darkness falls on all partners.

So, why is the gym a strategy, you ask? I'm trying to get you to a place where you can see how torment works everywhere. There's no place where torment gets turned away at the door. Torment has VIP access. Torment is king.

Now, back to the gym. There are four strategies I'm going to personally train you in today. And, because the fourth one is so great, I'm going to save it for Today's Tactic.

Let's begin. First, as you know, your partner is insanely insecure, so you must get him to step on the scale every time he goes to them gym. No matter what number populates on the scale, you must twist it. You must also whisper every time he walks by a mirror so that he turns and looks at himself. You must tell him to only use machines that face a mirror so that he can see himself. You want the gym to represent a place of insecurity at all times. He must bel*eve there is no place where he can escape his thoughts.

Second and third, you must also focus his attention on Jim & Jen. You want comparison and lust to saturate his mind at all times. Just like he won't go without his D-vice, he won't cancel his gym membership either.

Know that he bel*eves this new form of torment will only last for a season, and that he'll eventually overcome it as well.

xxx†xxx

Today's Tactic: More. Whisper to him to lift more weight. Whisper to him to run more. Whisper to him to workout more days. The more you can get him to do, the bigger the chance you have of him injuring himself. That's our goal with this tactic. Injury. We l*ve injuries. Injuries give us more access to a deeper level of tormenting.

See, we can't literally cause the injury ourselves; we can only suggest, deceive, and trick him into harming himself or others. This goes all the way back to the man whose fam*ly and servants were killed by his enemies. We didn't kill his fam*ly or servants, but we did deceive the man into thinking his G*d did the killing.

To this day, many partners are still deceived about what happened to this man. All this to say, seek first to whisper the thoughts which lead to injuries.

SINcerely,
SINister
CEO • PsyD, EdD

Day 28:
Death Groups

Good morning, %%First Name%%. I h*pe you are looking forward to today's strategy. You will have to be super careful when using this strategy with your partner. If you've been able to keep your partner in church, then now is the time for him to be called up to the community big leagues, which means you will have to be on your A-game.

Today is the day that your partner joins a death group at his church. I realize his church uses the term l*fe group, but we hate that term and aim to keep l*fe from happening. So, cease the tormenting at church when they are announcing these groups. You need him to focus during the announcement so he can hear their ignorant infomercial. Immediately after their sales pitch ends, whisper statements of guilt in order to have him join. Once he joins, the end begins.

The goal of the death group strategy is to fracture every possible relationship that he starts to build so that he never thinks about building another relationship, especially with partners he refers to as bel*evers. From the moment he arrives at his death group, begin to slowly turn on the faucet of assumptions. If he's like most partners, you can get him to think his assumptions are int*ition and disc*rnment. This will allow him to build a strong case about each defendant in his community courtroom without cognitively detecting what's going on.

Note: Assumptions never cause partners to prematurely pull the plug, because at the core of an assumption is self-doubt.

As he drives home, highlight a partner he feels threatened by, and begin stacking one assumption on top of the other until he is on the edge of hatred. Now, when your partner returns the following week, begin attacking him on the drive over. You want him to arrive at the group carrying a sweet dessert and a bitter attitude. When he walks through the door, make sure he's on high alert with last week's partner while you begin to whisper terrible thoughts to him about a less fortunate partner who is there.

This time on his drive home, you will now have two ways to torment him simultaneously with assumptions.

xxx†xxx

Today's Tactic: The quickest way you can cause disharmony and dissension in his death group, is by getting him to share his strong opinions on questions that cannot be answered (Do you think Judas went to h*aven? Do you bel*eve once sav*d, always sav*d? Did G*d really forsake His son?). When his opinion is voiced, the group will begin to divide and different camps will be established. Of course, this division doesn't happen physically, but it happens mentally over time. Partners can't help but choose a side. This type of division is a perfect example of why there is nothing new under the sun. This has been going on forever.

In fact, this tactic is why we are where we are now as opposed to the place we departed from in the beginning.

So, shove this timeless tactic into his mind. Persuade him with logical thoughts. Provide him with elegant speech. Convince him to think for himself since his thoughts come from you. Whatever you do, don't give him a quiet moment during his death group where he could possibly seek first the counsel of his G*d.

SINcerely,
SINister
CEO • PsyD, EdD

Week 5

Day 29:
The Offensive OS

%%First Name%%, we are down to our final four strategies. These four are heavily concentrated, and are only to be used if the previous strategies begin to wane. That being whispered, let's hop into today's strategy.

It's taken us centuries to work out the bugs, but we are proud to announce the latest offensive version of our OS is now available for download. You can begin the update on your partner while he sleeps. The following day, when he has rebooted, you will cause him to be hypersensitive to almost every word spoken by other partners.

He won't realize that it's a choice to be offended because we will have other frequencies in place that reinforce the offensive operating system. You must teach him to offend with words and to also be offended by words. As this happens, your partner will be forced to curb his thoughts and carefully choose his words, and guess who will be providing him with new thoughts? Yes! You.

If this strategy goes as well as we have forecasted, your partner could mentally commit himself within a matter of weeks. The byproducts of offense are so lethal, we aren't even sure how maniacally sensitive partners might become. The worst we can h*pe for by creating such a sensitive society would be to see partners lose their jobs or get publicly shamed over something as granular as a few spoken words. Imagine this strategy at scale!

So, let Sensitivity and Offense do their thing. You can start by telling your partner to watch the news, read the paper, subscribe to podcasts, and watch documentaries on YouTube so that he can be in-the-know about the current times and cultural climate. This will give him a sense of responsibility, and provide him with the offensive ammo he needs for when he's around other partners.

Be sure to distract him when he stumbles upon good news as well. You can do this by whispering thoughts of doubt, suspicion, and cynicism. Over time, he will begin to identify with certain groups and acronyms that he's learned about through his ~~medium~~ media. Shortly after that, you can cause division to grow just like you did in his death group.

xxx†xxx

Today's Tactic: It's more important that you get your partner to be offended than for him to offend because it's only natural that offended partners offend partners.

Let me give you a beautiful visual for this tactic. When offense is properly administered, it ends up looking like a colony of cannibalistic lizards that only feed on each other's tails.

Here's how you can cause the feeding to happen. Burrow deep into your partner's mind, and locate a wound of insecurity that never fully healed. Then, begin to scratch it open with the dull knife of fear. After fear has reopened the wound, douse it with doubt. This will cause your partner to mentally recoil thus putting him in a state of defense.

When your partner falls into defense, his new operating system will serve up and loop offense.

SINcerely,
SINister
CEO • PsyD, EdD

Day 30:
Discount Celebrations

%%First Name%, Hooray! Today is a frigid day to celebrate. We are starting to see more and more partners' l*ve grow cold. This means you are doing a good job. As I mentioned in the previous email, we are almost at the end of our campaign. But, don't worry; we will have more email campaigns down the road.

Today's strategy gives me a reason to celebrate because it will help you be able to demean and discount your partner's celebrations. I'll explain. While the majority of your work is based on tormenting your partner, there's one outlying scenario that runs the risk of causing him to celebrate with other partners even though his personal world is upside down. The scenario I'm referring to is when a partner claims that he has given his l*fe to j*sus. Whenever you hear a partner proclaim this madness, you will also see all the other partners celebrate with him as well. It's chaos. I hate to admit the following, but there's nothing we can do to keep partners from proclaiming with their mouth once they bel*eve in their h*art. Do not allow him to celebrate.

Our preferred method has always been to perform mental magic so partners won't celebrate with other proclaiming partners. And, that's what we desire for you to do as well. You must discount every salv*tion celebration in your partner's mind. You must also discount celebration in general. The best way to discount celebration is with denial and doubt. You must plant tares wherever you see celebration growing. Celebration has to be choked out.

Again, comb through his Book of lies and memorize all the places where salv*tion is mentioned because salv*tion breeds celebration. Whenever a celebration takes place, drop a seed of doubt into your partner's mind using a sentence from his Book of lies that disproves the partner's perceived salv*tion. Then, your partner will backtrack, reflect, pause, and not celebrate.

At the same time, you need to turn off all tormenting so he will have a moment of pe*ce. This will cause him to feel rightly justified in his assumption. Repeat this behavior with all celebrations. The more he discounts celebrations, the less j*y he will have.

xxx†xxx

Today's Tactic: Besides salv*tions, the other celebrations we despise come from mir*cles. We never know where mir*cles come from or when they are about to happen. We know it has something to do with a right hand and left hand, but we've yet to figure it out. Until we do, you must discount all mir*cles as well. The best way to discount a mir*cle is with judgment. The moment the mir*cle arrives, have him cut it down and dissect it. For example, if your partner hears of a generous donation that was made so that a shelter could be built for the homeless, tell him the nonprofit won't last. If a widow is completely delivered from alcohol abuse, tell him she's bound to relapse. If an innocent prisoner who was serving a l*fe sentence is released, educate him on recidivism rates. Anything and everything that could be celebrated must be discounted.

SINcerely,
SINister
CEO • PsyD, EdD

Day 31:
Held in Contempt

%%First Name%%, good morning. Today, I'm going to share a strategy with you that by itself has the power to grow on its own once planted. This weapon should never be used on the strangers your partner meets, nor with everyday acquaintances. This weapon is strictly reserved for those whom he has grown to l*ve. If somehow he has grown to l*ve multiple partners, shift your focus primarily to his worthless wife.

The most important thing to know about this weapon is that its' effects must never see the l*ght of day. It must always remain within. Your partner must hold in contempt. Contempt is the cancerous tool that causes your partner to despise and dishonor his wife over a period of time. Planting contempt is our version of partner pregnancy. Once contempt is conceived, it's only a matter of time before destruction is birthed and mass casualties are left behind. One of the best times to impregnate your partner with contempt is when he and his wife are having a miscommunication. You must be laser-focused while studying both partners as they childishly spray venom back and forth at each other. It's in this glorious heat of the moment when you begin to channel the carriers of contempt through the wall of his mind. All we need is for one single swimmer to enter. Once this happens, the job is done. You can now return to your usual mode of tormenting.

Just like with partner pregnancy, you won't see contempt growing initially, but you will see contemptuous facial expressions on your partner's face when he converses with his wife. This is a great sign.

Now, unfortunately, I must warn you there have been times in history when contempt has been aborted. Again, we do not know why this happens or how to stop it from happening, all we can do is start the process over again. If this happens with your partner, don't sweat it. We have a library of how-to strategies for impregnating your partner with contempt.

xxx†xxx

Today's Tactic: Deep down, most married partners have a self-serving and conditional l*ve towards each other. If you can get your partner to see all of the selfish things his scornful wife does, you can use his pride as a channel to send the carriers of contempt on their way.

When they have any conversation, and she shrieks a first person pronoun, begin to repeatedly whisper these pronouns in his ear. By the end of the conversation, he will have a blank look on his face, which will annoy her because she'll assume he wasn't listening, but in fact he was just processing all of the selfish pronouns she somehow strung together. This will create either a miscommunication or an argument.

If we can get both to happen, his mind will ovulate.

SINcerely,
SINister
CEO • PsyD, EdD

Day 32:
Undetected in The Desert

%%First Name%%, today is the day. Today is the final day. Today is the day that our lord has made where I get to lead you into our promise land known as The Desert. Today is the day where your partner's progress ends. The reason why we save the worst tactic for last as opposed to the beginning, is because we have to let the mental clay of pride and arrogance dry over a period of time.

Here we go. The very worst thing your partner can do before leaving earth to join us, is plant or water a seed. Think about it. What good does it do for you to torment your partner if while doing so he still plants a hundred seeds that lead to salv*tion?

Therefore, you must lead him into the desert of his mind. Just like when you caused him to discount celebrations, you must drastically discourage the act of planting seeds. This is why isolation is at the core of what we do. Partners who isolate hardly ever make any impact on other partners. It's like our Founder once said, "He who fishes on the couch never catches fish because he never left the house to get in the boat to cast the net." He also said, "How beautiful are the feet of the partners that are propped up at home!" If you can get your partner to isolate, remain quiet, judge others, hold in contempt, assume, and live in a constant state of insecurity and fear, then seeds of salv*tion will never be planted.

Another way to keep him from ever planting a seed is by focusing his attention on how other partners are planting seeds the incorrect way. Tell him there's only one way to plant a seed. Show him in his Book of lies the exact place where the one way to plant is located, and then tell him to research it heavily because he should study to show himself approved. Tell him to know his sentences in the Greek and to begin writing a book about it as well. You might be thinking this sounds dangerous, but don't worry, he won't ever finish writing the book. All of the previous tactics that you have poured into his mind will cause his cursor to eternally blink while the document collects digital dust. And, again, if he's at home with his feet propped up, day in and day out, then he's not planting on those days. That's a small victory for us.

Also, when a well-known partner who has planted thousands of seeds is exposed for secretly doing our work, make sure your partner focuses on the error as opposed to the seeds this partner previously sowed. If your partner focuses on the error, his mind will become infested with the maggots of jadedness. Any method of sowing that he sees which cannot be verified in his Book of lies, must be quickly questioned, scrutinized, and tossed aside.

xxx✝xxx

Today's Tactic: The best way to tempt your partner when he's in The Desert is by using the *If*-word (not the F-word) followed by a sentence from his Book of lies. If you do this, he will never see it coming.

However, if he ever counters your first whisper with tr*th, hit him again. If he counters a second time, hit him one last time. There has been only one Partner in all of history that ever conquered these three rounds of torment.

SINcerely,
SINister
CEO • PsyD, EdD

Gnash, I h*pe you enj*yed these emails, and that you now feel more equipped for your mission. I look forward to reading your replies: rr@rickyruss.com

*Dr. Robert Banks, a leading scholar of Lewis from Australia said, "Day after day of having the Devil as an interlocutor took its toll on Lewis." The subject matter was almost too dark for Lewis to write about and engage with in such an all-encompassing manner.

In what might have been his final interview, C.S. Lewis shared he didn't enjoy writing "The Screwtape Letters."

"They were dry and gritty going," he said. "At the time, I was thinking of objections to the Christian life, and decided to put them into the form, 'That's what the devil would say.' But making goods 'bad' and bads 'good' gets to be fatiguing."

*Article on https://jimdaly. focusonthefamily.com/three-things-might-not-know-c-s-lewis-screwtape-letters/

xxx†xxx

As for me, it was quite easy to write about this way of thinking. The rough draft took me less than three weeks to write. All I had to do was reflect on my past, and a little bit on my present since Gnash still whispers to me.

I could've comfortably sat back and fine-tuned these emails until the day they were perfect, but I knew I'd be playing into the words of Gnash *IF* I did so.

Cover image:
File ID: 42262206
https://www.dreamstime.com/gleighly_info
Gleighly
www.dreamstime.com

Made in the USA
Middletown, DE
22 March 2023